Craft Ideas for 8 year Olds   (Paper Town – Create Your Own Town Using 20 Templates)

20 full-color kindergarten cut and paste activity sheets designed to create your own paper houses. The price of this book includes 12 printable PDF kindergarten workbooks

PASSWORD FOR BONUS BOOKS IS ON PAGE 16

BONUS BOOKS - website download details

https://www.westsuffolkcbt.net/product/craft-1/

https://www.westsuffolkcbt.net/product/craft-2/

https://www.westsuffolkcbt.net/product/craft-3/

https://www.westsuffolkcbt.net/craft-4/

CPSIA information can be obtained
at www.ICGtesting.com
Printed in the USA
BVHW052035170619
551189BV00016B/1518/P